THE Big Blue THING ON THE Hill

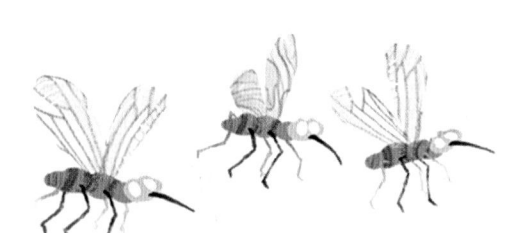

To a small boy called Or and a smaller girl called Shir, with all my love.
And also with thanks to big kids Mandy, Libby and Mike
for holding my hands all the way up the hill... Y.Z.

A TEMPLAR BOOK

First published in the UK in 2014 by Templar Publishing,
an imprint of The Templar Company Limited,
Deepdene Lodge, Deepdene Avenue, Dorking, Surrey, RH5 4AT, UK
www.templarco.co.uk

ISBN 978-1-84877-772-9 (hardback)
ISBN 978-1-84877-760-6 (paperback)

Edited by A. J. Wood & Libby Hamilton

Printed in China

THE BiG BLUE THiNG ON THE HiLL

templar publishing

ZZZZZZ

Far away from the city, in the middle of the Great Forest, was a special place called **HOWLING HILL**. In the day it was mostly peaceful and quiet, because all the animals were asleep.

But at night the forest really came **alive**...

Out came the foxes and the weasels. Out came the boars and the badgers.

The bears lumbered out of their lairs to practise their **growlings**.

The wolves crept out of their dens to practise their **HOWLING**.
And all was well in the Great Forest at the foot of Howling Hill.
Until one night something **TERRIBLE** happened...

First there was a rumble,
then there was a ROAR
and finally a terrifying sight appeared,
right on top of Howling Hill.

"It's a meteorite!" said the bears.
"It's a spaceship!" said the wolves.
"It's trouble!" said the foxes.
And the foxes were **right**.

So they all went to hide in the
Great Forest, hoping that the trouble
would soon be gone.

Early next morning, the animals crept back to the foot of Howling Hill, but the trouble was STILL there...

"It's a big blue elephant!" said the weasels (who had plainly never seen an elephant before). "It's a big blue dinosaur!" said the badgers (equally birdbrained).

"It's a **BIG BLUE THING**," said the foxes (who were right again). And everyone agreed that it seemed to be awake and should probably be left well alone until it fell asleep.

"Perhaps we can frighten it away?" suggested the wolves, when the animals returned at dusk. They waited for the moon to come up and then they howled and **HOWLED** and **HOWLED** at the Big Blue Thing...

"Let us have a go!" suggested the bears.
So they growled and **growled** and **GROWLED**
at the Big Blue Thing...

GRROOOWWLL

GRROOOWWLL

But it did not
move, even one inch.

GRROOOWWLL

"Perhaps we can nudge it back down the hill?" suggested the boars.

They **huffed** and **puffed** as they PUSHED and SHOVED with all their might...

But the Big Blue Thing still didn't move, not even the tiniest bit.

"How about burying it?" suggested the foxes.
So the foxes, the badgers and the weasels gathered
around and they **dug** and **dug** and
then **DUG** some more.

But, just as it looked as though their
plan might work...

the Big Blue Thing made a noise.

"IT'S WAKING UP!" shouted the animals. And they all fled back to the safety of the Great Forest.

No one knew what to do next, so they called a general forest meeting to ask the Wise Owls what to do about the problem of the Big Blue Thing.

And after some **hoots** and **toots** and rather loud **WHOOPS,** the Wisest Old Owl announced a most cunning plan...

The plan had **four** very important steps,
as the Wisest Old Owl explained:

" 1. We summon the help of our **smallest** forest friends –
the bees and wasps, midgies and mozzies
(and a snake or two for good measure).

2. We ask them all (nicely)
to form a **BIG BUG FLYING SQUAD**.

3. We wait until dawn.
Then, when the Big Blue Thing starts to
wake up, the squad must go **inside**
the mouth of the beast.

4. They must **whizz** and **buzz** and **BUZZ** and **whizz**
(and if necessary nip and sting). Then, in my experience,
it won't be long before that Big Blue Thing is long gone."

By the time the sun was
peeking over the top of Howling Hill,
a **big** black cloud of the forest's finest bugs
(and a snake or two for good measure)
were ready to **ZOOM** in.

They **whizzed** and **buzzed**
as they flew and crawled through every crack,
right inside the Big Blue Thing...

It didn't take long before it was
clear that the Wise Old Owl had been right!
With a **roar** and a **rumble**, the Big Blue Thing
turned tail and fled, back down Howling Hill
and away, away to wherever it had come from.

And all the while the animals screeched and GROWLED,
roared and howled, snuffed and huffed
and generally made such a HULLABALOO
it was heard for miles and miles.

HOOOWWLL

HiiiSSS

After that things got back to normal
in the Great Forest at the foot of Howling Hill,
and every day was peaceful and
quiet ONCE MORE.

Until one fine night...